My Family

David Beckett

ROSEN
COMMON CORE
READERS

Rosen Classroom™

New York

Published in 2013 by The Rosen Publishing Group, Inc.
29 East 21st Street, New York, NY 10010

Book Design: Michael Harmon

Photo Credits: Cover, pp. 5, 7,11 Yuri Arcurs/Shutterstock.com; p. 9 Gelpi/Shutterstock.com; p. 13 Sophie Louise Phelps/Shutterstock.com; p. 15 Lucian Coman/Shutterstock.com.

ISBN: 978-1-4488-8683-8
6-pack ISBN: 978-1-4488-8684-5

Manufactured in the United States of America

CPSIA Compliance Information: Batch #WS12RC: For further information contact Rosen Publishing, New York, New York at 1-800-237-9932.

Word Count: 24

Contents

This is my mother.

5

This is my father.

7

This is my brother.

This is my sister.

11

This is my grandpa.

13

This is my grandma.

15

Words to Know

brother

father

grandma

grandpa

mother

sister

Index

16